Star Baby

Written by
Sylvestra Throckmorton

Illustrated by
Sylvestra Throckmorton,
Candie Scoles
and Benjamin Fritsch

Star Baby
By Sylvestra Throckmorton - 1st Ed.

Illustration by Sylvestra Throckmorton,
Candie Scoles and Benjamin Fritsch

Graphic Design & Layout by
Infinite-Creations.com

ISBN 0-9761723-1-3

Printed in Korea

Publisher
A.S. Greene & Company
1828 Kings Highway
Lincoln Park, MI 48146

To my precious daughters,
Marissa-Tate and Mayci-Rose,

This is the story of how we came to be
together as a family.

All my love,
Momma

A special thanks to the friends and family
that support and love us.

A very heartfelt thanks to Bernice and Eston Goodell
for stepping in as the Grandparents that my children
would have never had.

Eternal gratitude to Grandma Madeleine Goldstein
for also stepping in as "Grandma"
but mostly thank you for all that you do for us.
We love you!

A big thanks to Carol Coccia and Carol Perrott

Thank you, Grammy Angel and Papa Boy for making
all of this possible.

There once was a lady named Annie Cabannie.
She had lots of cats but not enough family.
She had a nice house, good friends, and her Dad.
She should have been happy but sometimes felt sad.

"Maybe a Baby is just what we're missin'.
Somewhere there's a cute one that we should be kissin'!"

Up in the sky, on a Star floating by,
Was a Baby as cute as could be.

"Can't wait to be picked as somebody's Baby,
And find the family that's just right for me."

"OH GURRY, FURRY, NURD MUFFINS!!
I want a family with babies and cousins!"

Each night to the stars, Annie would gaze,
Up she'd look and she would say,

"Star Baby, no matter where you are,
No matter where you land,
I will find you, kiss you, and hold your sweet hand.
I hope you hear this little plea
To just hold on 'til we can be
Together as a family."

Grammy Angel, Annie's mom in the sky,
Said down to Annie from way upon high,

"I will lead you to your little girl,
Even if it's way 'round the world,
So just hold on and you will see,
You will have your family."

Annie went to Morning Star,
For they found babies near and far.

"Please write here and over there,
Up and down and everywhere."

"GEES-O-PIZZA! I've told all I know!"

The lady then asked, "Who will help Baby grow?"

"First and foremost, is my dad, Papa Boy.
He sings and he dances. He'll bring Baby joy!
He's the family favorite, makes everyone laugh.
He loves bouncing babies who grab at his cap."

There are aunties and cousins,
And friends by the dozens
Who are doctors and teachers and such.
They'll hug her and squeeze her.
They'll kiss her and please her.
They'll love her and teach her so much."

Day after day, she fought back the blues,
Thought she'd go crazy before she got news!

"DANGY WANGY, ELEPHANT BEEKS!!!
Waiting months and waiting weeks!
I'm sure that a family is just what I'm missin'.
Somewhere there's a Mommy that I should be kissin'!"

Annie phoned the folks at the agency.
They said, "We've got pictures and you might see,
A Baby for your family!"

"I'm stuck here at work
And can't leave until four.
Could you please leave the pictures
Taped onto your door?"

The day seemed endless, she needed to race
To see Baby pictures.
Would she know the right face?

"Don't worry, Mommy, I'm waiting and ready.
Just look for a picture with me and my Teddy."

One magical smile and that's all it took.
She picked out Star Baby with one little look!

"And now that I know who my Baby will be,
I feel I must travel immediately.
I'll go to the spot where she fell to earth,
Antigua, Guatemala, the place of her birth."

"Oh no, you can't go!
Everything must be just so.
There's a paper to sign and then another.
It takes a lot to be a new mother."

"HA CHA CHILLY CHEEKS!!! I'll go nuts waiting weeks.
I'll fix up her room with duckies and such.
She's sure to know that she's loved very much."

"HA CHA CHILLY CHEEKS!!! I'll go nuts waiting weeks.
I'll pack more things for me and my Bear.
I hope Mommy likes them cause we plan to share."

"Star Baby, the same moon and stars
Shine down on us both.
They carry my message,
My sincere heartfelt oath
To find you and love you.
I promise we'll be
Together real soon
As a new family."

"I see Papa Boy in his silly old hat.
I can't wait to meet him and all of those cats!
Jump on a plane. Do whatever it takes.
I'm ready to travel for goodness sakes!"

Out of the blue and too good to be true,
Annie could leave the next day.
To bring back Star Baby
To her new home in Redford,
Where she'd happily learn, grow, and play.

Annie sat on the plane, scared out of her wits.
She wondered and worried,
"Would it be a good fit?
There's no turning back now, I must be brave.
Let me be a good mommy."
From her heart she would pray.

Dressed in white, a most beautiful sight,
Star Baby could finally go home.
Together they'd fly
Cross the world through the sky,
And never again feel alone.

Annie Cabannie named her new daughter Frannie,
Then left to go home on their flight.
Peacefully sleeping, no wiggles, no weeping,
Annie held Frannie tighter than tight.

Family and friends waited to greet her.
All were excited to hug her and meet her.
A party with presents, what a surprise!
And kisses from Papa, the very best prize!

After a while as her Star Baby grew,
Annie felt feelings that she never knew.
Annie and Frannie grew closer each day.
Hugging her Baby, Annie would say,

"I've never known a love quite like this.
Nothing as great or as sweet as your kiss.
I'm better and braver than I knew I could be.
Nothing means more than you do to me."

They loved happily ever after, well almost you see...
Each wanted a Baby for more family!

"OH CHIMEE CHAUNGAS!!!!
There's still something missin'.
Somewhere there's a sister that we should be kissin'."

So Annie Cabannie and her little girl, Frannie,
Nightly lifted their eyes to the sky.
"Dear Grammy Angel, your first match was perfect,
So there's something we'd like you to try.
We need a sister to add to our midst,
We'll love her and feed her
And make sure she's kissed."
And when they were certain that Grammy had heard,
Together they sang out these comforting words."

"Star Baby, no matter where you are,
No matter where you land,
We will find you, kiss you,
And hold your sweet hand.
We hope you hear this little plea to just hold on
Til we can be together as a family."

Night after night, they'd count planes overhead.
They had a great view from a place by the bed.

"Someday in a plane and too tiny to see.
Bringing home Baby, will be you, will be me!"

One long year later
We finally got news
To whip out the diapers
And buy baby shoes!!

Love at first sight.
Wildest dreams do come true!
Jannie became
Little Star Baby Two!!

Thanks, Grammy Angel! Great job again!